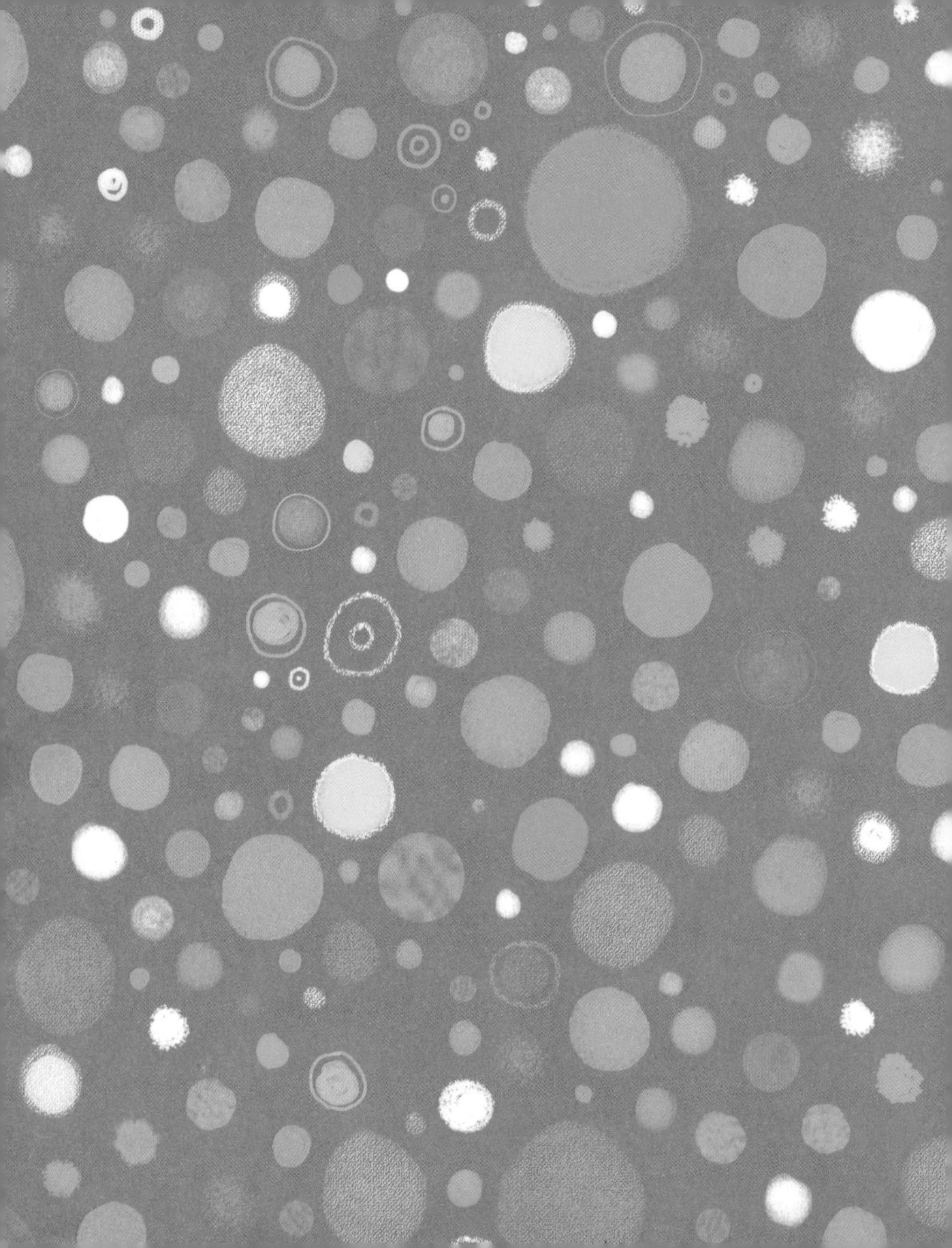

Big Sisters are the BEST

by Fran Manushkin

illustrated by Kirsten Richards

PICTURE WINDOW BOOKS

a capstone imprint

There's somebody new in our family.

It's a baby!

Our baby is little, and I am big.

I am a big sister!

I sleep in a big-sister bed.

Our baby sleeps in a crib.

Little babies are
LOUD and a
little smelly.

When our baby cries, I know why.
The baby's saying,
"It's time for a new diaper."
Or "I'm hungry."

Little babies drink bottles.

Big sisters eat **cupcakes**!

Big sisters are a big help!

Pat-pat-pat — I burp the baby . . .

. . . and put on socks, and hug our baby,
but not too hard.

Sssh! Now our baby is sleeping.

I tell Mommy, "It's hard to be quiet."

“I know,” she says. “We can play quiet games inside or noisy games outside.”

Big sisters can **yell**,

and turn somersaults,

and swing upside down.

Once I was little, like the baby.
See the pictures? Mommy and Daddy
took good care of me.

When they are busy with our baby,
I take care of mine!

Later, it's big-sister time.
Mommy and I paint pictures.
Daddy and I **fly**!

I tell the baby, “One day, you’ll be big enough to play with me.”
Our baby smiles and holds my finger tight!

“Big sisters are the best,” Mommy says.

I am big, for sure!

But I’m still the right size for snuggling on Mommy’s lap . . .

. . . and riding on Daddy's back.

At our house, there are plenty of hugs
and kisses for everyone —
especially for a **big sister!**

Published by Picture Window Books
A Capstone Imprint
1710 Roe Crest Drive
North Mankato, MN 56003
www.capstonepub.com

Library of Congress Cataloging-in-Publication Data
Manushkin, Fran.
Big sisters are the best / by Fran Manushkin; illustrated by Kirsten Richards.
p. cm.
Summary: The story follows a young girl as she helps to care for the new baby in her family.
ISBN 978-1-4048-7138-0 (library binding)
1. Infants—Juvenile fiction. 2. Sisters—Juvenile fiction. 3. Familie—Juvenile fiction. [1. Babies—Fiction. 2. Brothers and sisters—Fiction. 3. Family life—Fiction.] I. Richards, Kirsten, ill. II. Title.

PZ7.M3195Bh 2012
813.54—dc23 2011029605

Designer: Emily Harris
Creative Director: Heather Kindseth
Production Specialist: Danielle Ceminsky

Printed in the United States of America in North Mankato, Minnesota.
062013 007346R